Seahorse Stars

Seahorse Stars

The First Pearl

Zuzu Singer

Illustrated by Helen Turner

Meet the Pearlies

Fun and friendly CAMMIE is
a vivid pink seahorse who dreams
of becoming a Seahorse Star.

Shy but
sweet
CORA is
a pretty
pink seahorse
with pale
pink stripes.

Bossyboots
CORINETTA is
a golden seahorse
with a snooty
upturned nose.

Cammie's
best friend
JESS is
a born
storyteller.
She is a bright
bluey-green.

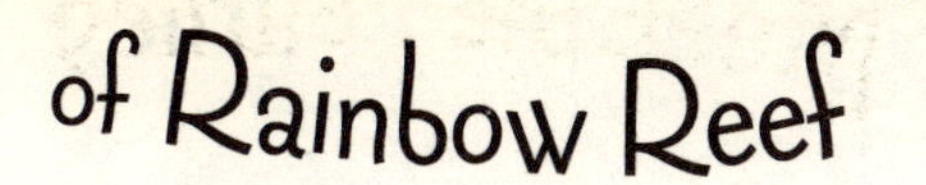

# of Rainbow Reef

Pale-green
MISS SWISH
is firm but fair
as the elegant
leader of
the Pearlies.

Brainbox BREE
knows all the answers!
She is purple with lovely
lavender fins.

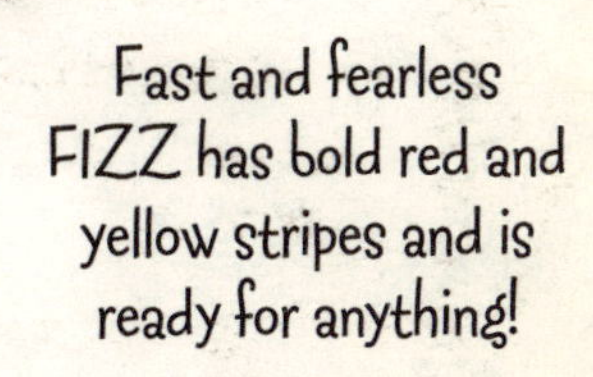

Fast and fearless
FIZZ has bold red and
yellow stripes and is
ready for anything!

Rainbow Reef
Coral Tower
Seahorse City
Eelgrass forest
Palace
Sandy Cove
Pearlie Pavilion
Cammie's House
Pink Sand Plains
Coral Caves

Camping Caves
N
W
E
S
Lagoon
Town Hall
Library
Crystal Caves
White Sands
Primary School
Whirlpool
Danger!
The Deep

Seahorse Stars is dedicated to every child who loves to read...including you!

First published in the UK in 2011 by Usborne Publishing Ltd., Usborne House, 83-85 Saffron Hill, London EC1N 8RT, England. www.usborne.com

A CIP catalogue record for this book is available from the British Library.

FMAMJJASOND/11 02339/1

ISBN 9781409520245 Printed in Reading, Berkshire, UK.

Chapter One

Cammie Sunbeam could hardly contain her excitement as she and her father swam through the warm waters of Rainbow Reef. "Hurry, Dad!" she urged, darting in front of him and flicking her bright pink tail. "All the other seahorses will be there by now."

Her father chuckled as they glided past a

shoal of shiny silverfish. "I think *someone* is being a bit impatient," he said with a grin.

Cammie held back a groan. Her father could always be counted on for a joke...even when Cammie didn't think anything was funny! It would be awful if she were the last seahorse to turn up on such an important day.

When the pink coral of the Pearlie Pavilion came into view, Cammie caught her breath. She had never seen so many seahorses in her life! Every girl she knew from White Sands Primary seemed to be there, plus lots more from other schools besides. Each young seahorse was accompanied by a parent. The crowd made a rainbow of colours as they swam in front of the Pavilion, laughing and chatting.

"See, Miss Worry? We've plenty of time yet," teased Cammie's father. Unlike Cammie and her mum, Cammie's father was a rich, vivid blue, and his dancing eyes were full of laughter.

"I suppose," admitted Cammie with a sheepish smile. Even so, it would be nice if her father hurried sometimes! Suddenly Cammie spotted her best friend in the crowd. "Jess," she called, bobbing up and down. "Over here!"

A pretty blue-green seahorse swam quickly over to them. "Cammie!" she squealed, giving Cammie a hug with her tail. "Oh, isn't it wavy? We're going to be Pearlies at last!"

Cammie nodded. "And you know what comes after the Pearlies," she said eagerly.

"*Seahorse Stars!*" cried both girls together. They spun in place, twirling their tails. The Seahorse Stars were the waviest club in Rainbow Reef – but before you could be one you had to first be a Pearlie, and earn your pearls. Cammie could hardly wait to begin.

"Well, you'd better not be late for your first meeting if you want to be Seahorse Stars some day," said her father. "Look, they're getting started!"

Cammie's heart leaped as she saw it was true: the Pearlie leaders were heading inside the Pavilion, followed by streams of children. "Bye, Dad," she said, nudging against him and fluttering her fins. “Wish me luck. The next time you see me, I’ll be a Pearlie!”

“I’ll be back later to collect you.” Her dad smiled. “And I don’t think you’ll need any luck, Cammie – you’ll do just fine!”

Even so, Cammie and Jess linked tails tightly as they swam towards the hole in the pink coral that was the doorway. Cammie held her breath as they joined the other young seahorses heading inside. What would the Pavilion be like? She had wondered so many times, and now she would finally see it for herself.

The two friends glided through the doorway, and Cammie gasped as they emerged into a huge, open space. It was like being inside a giant pink bowl!

The roof of the Pavilion was open to the warm currents of Rainbow Reef, while inside there was softly waving eelgrass, and gleaming white conch shells lying on the sand. Pearlie leaders darted this way and that through the water, organizing the children.

Cammie's eyes shone as she watched the busy scene. "I wonder which group we'll be in?" she whispered to Jess.

"I don't know," her best friend murmured back. "But I've heard that the Purple Corals have a really wavy time – I hope we're with them!"

Just then a tall, pale-green seahorse swam over to them, carrying a white shell in the crook of her tail. "Cammie Sunbeam and Jess Splash?" she asked, consulting a list of names written on the shell.

The two girls nodded shyly, and she smiled. "I'm Miss Swish, and I'm going to be your Pearlie leader. You're in my group, the Dancing Waves. Come along now, we're just getting started!"

Chapter Two

The Dancing Waves! Cammie repeated the name happily to herself as she and Jess swam after Miss Swish. She just knew already that it was going to be the most wonderful Pearlie group in the world.

Their new leader took them to a cosy corner of the Pavilion. Curved pink and white seashells served as chairs, with four other seahorse girls already seated on them. They looked up curiously as Cammie and Jess arrived.

Cammie smiled shyly at them, wondering what they were all like. She and Jess both went to White Sands Primary, and part of the fun of being a Pearlie would be meeting girls from other schools, like these.

Suddenly Jess stopped short. “Oh, no!” she hissed in Cammie’s ear. “Not *her* – I don’t believe it!”

“Who?” Cammie whispered back in alarm.

“Corinetta,” said Jess grimly, nodding towards a golden seahorse who sat a bit apart from the others. “She’s in my book club. Oh, this is just great!”

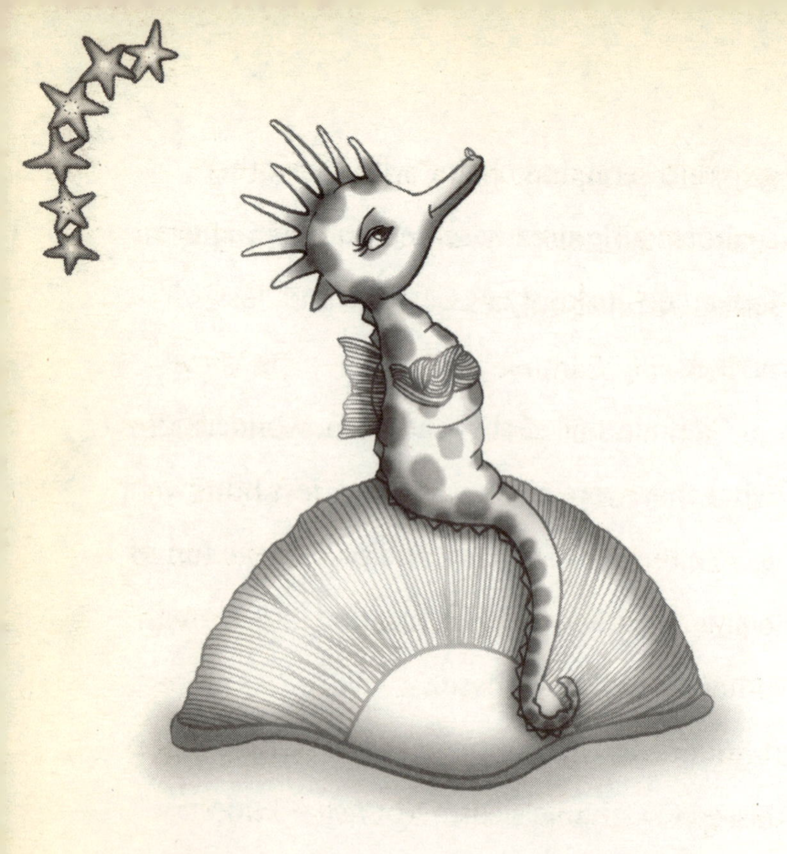

"Cammie, Jess, please take a seashell," called Miss Swish. She swam to the front of the Dancing Waves, where a piece of smooth grey slate was propped onto a coral stand.

Hastily, Cammie settled herself onto one of the remaining seashell seats. Jess sat next to her, still looking put out. Cammie glanced across at the golden seahorse, wondering what was so awful about her.

Suddenly Cammie realized that she knew one of the other girls, too. The purple seahorse with lavender fins was Bree, whose mother was a friend of Cammie's mother. Bree went to Pebble Primary and was extremely clever, with her nose always in a book. She was very nice, though, and Cammie was glad to see her. The two girls exchanged a smile as Miss Swish began to speak.

"Welcome to the Pearlie Pavilion," she said warmly. "By the end of this meeting you'll all be Pearlies...and on your way to becoming Seahorse Stars!" She paused impressively before continuing.

"Now, just in case any of you don't know, to become a Seahorse Star you must first earn six proficiency pearls." As Miss Swish spoke, she drew a curly question mark on the slate with a piece of chalk held in her tail.

"To earn your pearls, you must complete six tasks. These are kept secret until everyone starts working towards them, so that no Pearlie has an unfair advantage over the others. By the end of today, I shall reveal your first task."

All of the seahorses looked at each other excitedly. Cammie knew that once earned, the pearls were worn on the seahorses' natural crowns, so that everyone could see them. She could hardly wait to get her first one!

Miss Swish put the chalk down. "We'll take

the Pearlie Pledge shortly," she said. "First, though, I think it would be nice if we introduced ourselves to each other." She nodded at Corinetta. "Would you start us off, please? Tell us your name, and why you'd like to become a Pearlie."

The golden seahorse smirked. "I'm Corinetta," she said. "And I want to be a Pearlie because my mother and *all* my older sisters were ones, so of course I'll be a natural at it. Plus, the pearls are going to look really wavy on me." She tossed her head, showing off the unusually tall points of her crown.

Jess rolled her eyes. "What did I tell you?" she muttered to Cammie.

Miss Swish looked a bit taken aback. "Er… thank you, Corinetta. But I think you'll find that we don't become Pearlies *just* to wear the pearls! Next, please."

A seahorse with bold red and yellow stripes smiled at them. "Hi, I'm Fizz," she said cheerfully. "And I want to be a Pearlie because of all the great activities we get to do: camping, and deep-sea exploring, and all sorts! I can hardly wait."

Cammie couldn't help smiling back at her. At least Fizz seemed all right!

The next seahorse had long eyelashes, and pale pink stripes. "I'm Cora. And I want to be a Pearlie because...um..." She trailed off with a nervous giggle, shrugging her fins.

Miss Swish smiled. "Are you looking forward to exploring deeper waters, like Fizz?" she suggested. "Or perhaps finding out about Sea Safety?"

Cora blinked in alarm. "No, those both sound really scary! I don't know, I – I just want to be a Seahorse Star, that's all." She ducked her head.

"That's all right, Cora – I'm sure you'll gain a great deal from being a Pearlie," said Miss Swish kindly. "Now, who's next?"

Bree introduced herself. "I want to be a Pearlie because of all we can learn," she said. "There's a whole reef full of knowledge out there, and I want to discover everything I can about it!" She looked delighted at the thought.

Then it was Cammie's turn. She told the others her name. "I want to be a Pearlie because of everything the Seahorse Stars get to do," she said shyly. "They're always doing things to help the Reef, and I want to help it, too."

"A good answer," said Miss Swish with a smile. "Now, our last Dancing Wave." She motioned to Jess.

Jess introduced herself with a grin. "I want to be a Pearlie for all the reasons everyone's already said: exploring, and knowledge, and helping the Reef...but *especially* for wearing those pearls on my lovely crown!"

She tossed her head just like Corinetta had done. The others burst into laughter as the golden seahorse scowled. Even Miss Swish hid a smile. "All right, that's enough," she said. "I think it's time now for the Pearlie Pledge."

Wiping the slate clean with a bit of sponge, Miss Swish wrote down the pledge. Silence fell over the group as they gazed at the words that would officially make them Pearlies.

"Is everyone ready?" asked Miss Swish. Cammie nodded with the others, too thrilled to speak. "Good," said Miss Swish. "Then please swim forward, and join tails."

The seahorses formed a brightly-coloured cluster, linking their tails together.

"Now, repeat after me," said Miss Swish. "As a Pearlie, I promise to always do my best, to serve Rainbow Reef and all its creatures, to help other seahorses whenever I can, and to keep the Pearlie Rule."

Solemnly, Cammie said the words along with the rest of the Dancing Waves. The Pearlie Rule, she knew, was to think of others before herself, and to do a good turn every day. Her heart thudded with the seriousness of it.

When they had finished, Miss Swish looped a plaited seaweed necklace around each girl's neck. A small, pearl-coloured bead hung from each one. Cammie stared at hers in wonder.

"This bead represents your pledge, and shows everyone you're a Pearlie until you earn your first pearl," explained Miss Swish. She smiled warmly at them. "Congratulations, girls! Welcome to the Pearlies."

Chapter Three

During dinner that evening, Cammie couldn't stop talking about the Pearlies. Tigg and Stripe, her younger sister and brother, listened with open mouths as she described the Pearlie Pavilion.

"Cammie, will *I* get to be a Pearlie some day?" breathed Tigg. Cammie smiled and

nodded as she took a bite of her dad's delicious plankton stew.

"Of course! And then you'll get to wear a necklace like this one." She gazed proudly at the pearl bead that lay on her bright pink chest. Oh, this was the best day of her life!

The Sunbeam family's table was a large, round piece of coral, with five seashell seats around it. Pretty pebbles decorated the lavender walls of their coral home, and windows let in the shimmering sunlight that shone down through the bright blue water.

Cammie's mother smiled fondly at her from the head of the table. "Do you know yet what your first pearl is going to be?" she asked.

Cammie was very proud of her mum. She was the fastest seahorse in Rainbow Reef, and one of the guards who protected them all from danger. "Yes, Coral Camping!" she said eagerly. "Isn't it great that we're starting with something easy?"

Cammie's father spooned more food into her younger siblings' coral bowls. "Tigg, stop blowing bubbles in your stew," he said sternly.

Tigg got a wicked gleam in her eyes. "But Dad, I'm not Tigg, I'm Stripe," she said innocently. Tigg and Stripe were twins, and sometimes it was very hard to tell them apart!

"Yes, and I'm really Tigg!" sniggered Stripe. He pretended to be his sister, fluttering his fins and swishing his stripy tail. The little seahorses giggled, bobbing up and down in the water.

Cammie's father chuckled. "What do you mean, easy?" he asked Cammie, offering her

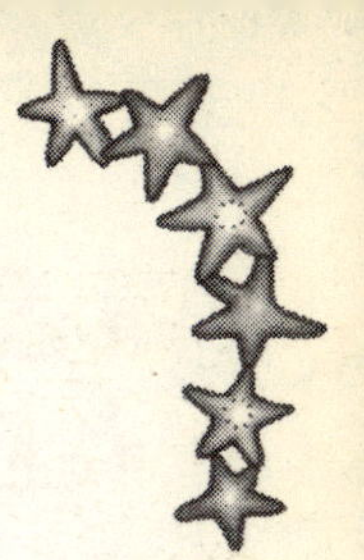

more stew. "Don't you have to set up a campsite to earn the camping pearl?"

"Yes, and catch and prepare our own dinner," explained Cammie. "But Dad, I've been camping loads of times with you and Mum – how hard can it be to do it myself?"

Cammie's parents exchanged a glance. Cammie thought she saw her mother hold back a smile. "I'm sure you'll do very well," said her mum gently. "But dear, if I were you, I'd pay attention to what Miss Swish tells you!"

The next few weeks seemed magical to Cammie. She wore her new necklace everywhere she went, earning admiring glances from younger girls. She did her best to uphold the Pearlie Rule every day, too –

though sometimes her younger siblings made it difficult!

Best of all, the Dancing Waves met once a week in the Pearlie Pavilion. Cammie loved swimming through the pink coral entrance with Jess, and sitting with the other girls while Miss Swish taught them the skills they needed to get their first pearl.

"The most important thing is to find a suitable cave," she said, drawing one on the slate. "It should be coral, of course, and not have any other creatures living in it. Now, who knows what you should do once you've found a cave?"

Corinetta fluttered her golden fins. "*I* know, Miss Swish. You should sweep it out, and then prepare a place to sleep." She looked smugly around her, as if expecting everyone to applaud.

Jess rolled her eyes. Cammie didn't blame her – the stuck-up seahorse was *so* irritating! Corinetta's presence in the Dancing Waves was the only thing that kept the Pearlies from being perfect.

"That's right," said Miss Swish. "Anything else?"

Bree waved a fin. "If it's dark, you should ask a phosphorescent fish to swim at the top of the cave, to give you light."

Cora gaped in confusion. "Phos-pho – a *what* fish?"

"Glow in the dark!" said Fizz, giving Cora a hearty nudge with her tail. "We'll need them down in the Deep, too, won't we, Miss Swish?" Fizz's eyes gleamed as Cora gulped in alarm.

Their leader nodded. "Yes, but that won't be for a long time to come. We have to master camping first! Now, remember, everyone, if you ever find yourself in a strange place, then the first thing you should do is build a campsite. Then you're all settled, and you can explore your new surroundings from there."

Despite herself, Cammie found her mind wandering. She knew it was important to pay attention...but this was all so easy! She'd far rather imagine getting her first pearl.

Gazing dreamily at the slate, Cammie saw herself in front of a crowd of Pearlies, trying to look modest as her friends all cheered. Miss Swish placed a single gleaming pearl onto Cammie's crown.

"Cammie, you're the best Coral Camper I've ever seen," praised the imaginary Miss Swish. "The others could learn a lot from you!"

Cammie sighed happily at her daydream. Suddenly she blinked in surprise. Beside her,

Jess was hissing her name, over and over again.

"Jess, hush, you'll get us into trouble!" whispered Cammie.

Her best friend blew out a frustrated breath. "You're already *in* trouble," she said in her normal voice. "That's what I've been trying to tell you!"

Cammie's crown went stiff with embarrassment as everyone burst into laughter. At the front, Miss Swish shook her pale green head. "Cammie, you weren't listening at all," she chided. "I just asked you a question about the right way to capture plankton."

"Sorry, Miss Swish," said Cammie guiltily. "I'll pay attention from now on."

Unexpectedly, Miss Swish smiled and put her chalk down. “Well, perhaps we’ve had enough lessons for the time being. How would you all like to take a camping trip for real?”

The water churned as the Dancing Waves twirled their tails in excitement.

“Oh, yes!”

“Miss Swish, that would be brilliant!”

Their Pearlie leader nodded. “All right, then. We’ll go on a practice camping trip next week, and see how you all do!”

Chapter Four

The next week Cammie felt very important as she arrived at the Pearlie Pavilion with a small rucksack on her back. It had everything in it she could possibly need – including Dad's fishing net, to catch her dinner with!

"Good luck with your practice campsite," said Dad, giving her a squeeze with his tail.

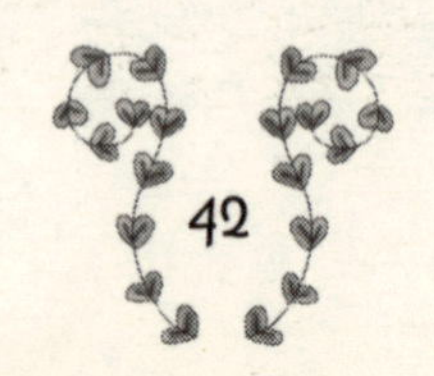

"And remember, pay attention to what Miss Swish says."

"I will, Dad," said Cammie excitedly.

Jess came swimming up, wearing a rucksack too. "Our first camping trip as Pearlies!" she exclaimed as she and Cammie swam towards the Pearlie Pavilion. Then she pulled a face. "I just hope Corinetta isn't too much of a pain."

Miss Swish was waiting outside with the rest of the Dancing Waves. "Is everyone here now?" she asked. She counted them quickly. "Good! Then let's go, girls – single swim."

She led the way off through the Reef, with the Dancing Waves swimming single file behind. Cammie gazed around her at the waving eelgrass and brightly-coloured coral.

Somehow Rainbow Reef looked very different now that she was setting off on such an important camping trip.

"I wonder where we're going?" fretted Cora. "I hope it's nowhere scary."

"Oh, don't be such a baby," scoffed Corinetta. "There's nothing scary about camping!"

Though Cammie agreed, she still thought Corinetta had been very rude. "Don't worry," she whispered to Cora over her shoulder. "Miss Swish wouldn't take us anywhere dangerous!"

The Dancing Waves swam for some time. They passed schools of fish and once even saw a giant sea turtle gliding along overhead! Finally they reached a large cluster of lavender coral.

"Here we are, girls," announced Miss Swish. "You're each to choose a cave and make your campsite. Good luck – and remember all I've told you!"

"Come on, Jess," said Cammie eagerly. "I see some really wavy caves over there!"

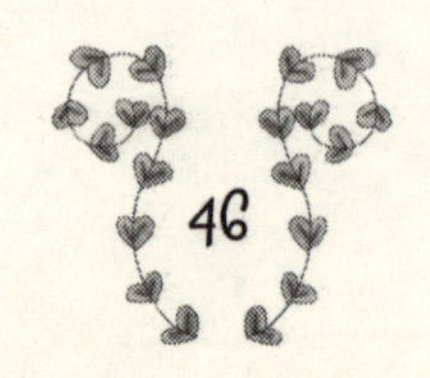

She pointed to a piece of coral a small distance away.

Jess frowned. "I don't know, Cammie... those caves look awfully dark. Miss Swish said a place with lots of sunlight is best."

"No, they're perfect!" insisted Cammie. "Trust me, Jess – I've been camping with my family loads of times."

Her friend didn't seem convinced. "We-ell...okay," she said finally.

Up close, the caves looked even more shadowy than before. Jess shook her head. "I'm really not sure about this. Miss Swish said—"

Cammie wasn't listening. "Look, here's a perfect cave!" she announced. "I'm going to take this one."

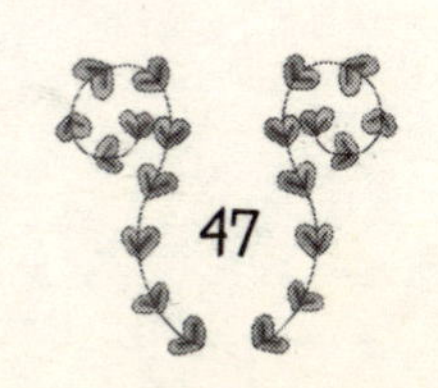

"Wait!" cried Jess in alarm. "You're supposed to study the sand outside first, to see if there are any—"

But Cammie had already shot inside. She looked around her happily. The cave was perfect – nice and cosy, with a white sand floor.

Then she gasped. What was *that*? In a dim corner, it almost looked as if there was a pair of eyes watching her. But no, that was silly, she told herself. It was probably just a couple of seashells.

Then Cammie shrieked as the seashells blinked!

"What are you doing here?" demanded a crab. He scuttled out towards her, clicking his claws. "This is *my* cave!"

Cammie gulped. "I – I'm sorry. I was just—"

"Just nothing!" huffed the crab. His eyes waved crossly on their stalks. "Get out this instant – and next time, knock!"

Cammie swam out as fast as she could, her face hot with embarrassment. Jess was waiting for her outside. "I tried to tell you!" she said. "Before you go into a cave, you're supposed to check the sand outside for footprints. See, look – crab tracks, going in and out!"

Cammie stared glumly down at the footprints. She had forgotten all about that! "I – I suppose these caves weren't such a good idea after all," she admitted. "Come on, let's go see where the others have gone."

But when they returned to the other section of coral, Cammie saw that all the best caves had been taken. Corinetta smiled out at them smugly from hers. "Where have you two been?" she called. "I've started cooking my plankton stew already!"

"Oh, so *that's* what that awful smell is," retorted Jess. Corinetta scowled and swished out of sight again.

"Sorry, Jess," said Cammie awkwardly. "We could have got much better caves, if it wasn't for me."

Jess shrugged her fins with a smile. "That's okay, it's only a practice. Come on – I'll take this one, and you can have that one."

When Cammie went into her cave, she looked around sadly. It was so small! Still, she could make it into a nice campsite if she tried. Now, what was the first thing Miss Swish had said to do? She wrinkled her brow, trying to recall.

Of course – prepare a place to sleep! Cammie sped out of her cave. Spotting some soft seaweed lying between a group of rocks, she quickly grabbed up a big tail-full.

In no time at all, she had returned to her cave and arranged the seaweed into a comfortable bed. She looked at it proudly. Now she just needed to cook her stew, and she'd be done!

No problem, thought Cammie. She took the fishing net from her rucksack and swam outside again. *I've watched Dad do this a million times!*

But the tiny fish just darted right past her. Cammie groaned with frustration. Dad made it look so easy! She glanced at Bree inside her cave, who was busy cooking her stew. Bree seemed to have loads of plankton. *How* had she done it?

The purple seahorse saw Cammie watching, and gave her a friendly look. "You're not holding the net right," she called. "Don't you remember what Miss Swish said? You're supposed to hold it really far away from you, so that the plankton swim in without realizing it."

"Oh," mumbled Cammie. This was awful – she was doing everything wrong! "Thanks, Bree," she said, trying to smile. Finally managing to catch a few plankton, she sighed as she returned to her own cave.

Camping was turning out to be a lot harder than she'd thought!

Chapter Five

Soon it was time for Miss Swish to inspect their campsites. The Pearlies all waited outside their caves as she examined each one. "Very nice, Bree," she said warmly. "Fizz, well done!"

Corinetta tossed her head as Miss Swish came to her cave. "I bet *mine's* the best!" she hissed to the other seahorses.

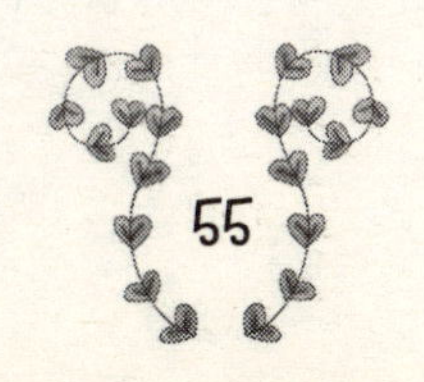

"Not bad, Corinetta," said Miss Swish as she came out of her cave. "But do try to be a bit tidier next time. Your bed looks like you've slept in it already!"

Corinetta's jaw dropped, and the other Pearlies sniggered. Then Cammie straightened quickly as Miss Swish swam up to her. "How did you do, Cammie?" asked the Pearlie leader with a smile.

"Oh – fine!" said Cammie, her cheeks turning red. She hoped Miss Swish hadn't noticed her going into the crab's cave!

She watched nervously as Miss Swish looked around her campsite. Finally her teacher turned to face her. "Cammie, are you sure this is the right sort of seaweed for a bed?" she asked gently.

"I – I think so," said Cammie in confusion. Was there more than one kind?

"No, this is deep-sea seaweed," explained Miss Swish. "You'd find it much too rough and uncomfortable to sleep on. You'll need to change it before bedtime. Remember, I told you to always use pale seaweed, not seaweed where the leaves are this dark!"

Dimly, Cammie remembered Miss Swish mentioning this. She bit her lip. She'd been too busy daydreaming to really pay attention.

"And you've forgotten to sweep the floor," continued Miss Swish. She showed Cammie all the little shells and pebbles on the ground. Cammie stared sadly at them. *How* could she have forgotten? That was the first thing you were supposed to do!

"Never mind! Where's your plankton stew?" asked Miss Swish, looking around.

Cammie hung her head. "I...I haven't had time to make it yet," she confessed. She knew this was because she'd wasted so much time in

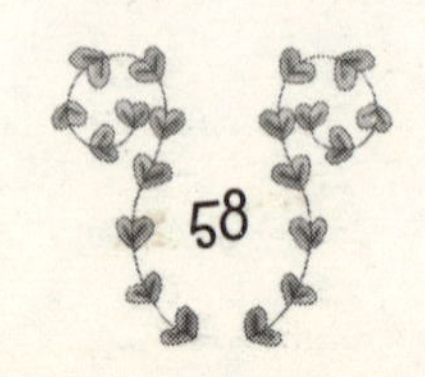

the crab's cave, and then taken so long to catch the plankton.

With the tip of her pale-green tail, Miss Swish lifted Cammie's chin up. Her eyes were kind. "Don't worry, it was only a practice! I'm sure you'll do much better when you try for your pearl in two weeks."

But Cammie still felt like crying as Miss Swish went on to the next cave. She had been so sure that she'd get everything right...and instead her campsite was the worst of anyone's.

To Cammie's surprise, she had a good time that night despite her worries. The Pearlies all gathered around a glowing piece of phosphorescent coral, tasting each other's stews and laughing.

Surprisingly, Cora's stew was the best. The pretty pink seahorse beamed as the others praised it. "I like to cook," she said shyly. "My older sister says it's the only thing in the Reef that doesn't scare me."

"Speaking of being scared, does anyone know any ghost stories?" asked Fizz eagerly.

"How childish," muttered Corinetta. Fizz scowled at her.

Miss Swish laughed. "It's not childish at all – I like a good ghost story myself! But not *too* scary," she warned. "I want everyone to be able to sleep tonight."

"*I* know one," said Jess suddenly. She grinned at Cammie. "It's called... *The Ghost of the Crotchety Crab!*"

Cammie held back a groan. She knew that

Jess would never tell anyone about her mistake with the crab's cave, but naturally her friend couldn't resist teasing her!

"The...the crotchety crab?" squeaked Cora. Her rosy cheeks went pale.

"Ooh, tell it, Jess!" cried Fizz, twirling her tail.

"Yes, do!" exclaimed Bree.

"Go on, Jess," said Cammie with a smile. The seahorses all settled down on bits of coral. Cammie thought that even Corinetta looked interested, though she tried to hide it!

It was quite dark by now, with the glowing coral the only light. A school of fish passed silently by overhead.

Jess cleared her throat. "Once upon a time...there was a Pearlie group called the Shining Waves," she said.

"Oh no, that's almost like us!" moaned Cora.

"Yes, and they all went camping together one night," continued Jess, her eyes sparkling. "And they stayed in a dark, lonely cave far out in the Reef. In the middle of the night they heard...*click, click, click!*"

With a whimper, Cora ducked her head down and clapped her fins over her ears. The other seahorses listened keenly.

"The noise grew louder," said Jess, waving her fins about. "CLICK, CLICK, CLICK! *CLICK, CLICK, CLICK!* It was the ghost of...the crotchety crab! He *hated* it when anyone came into his cave, and he said, *Whe-ere is my missing claw?* WHE-ERE IS MY MISSING CLAW?"

Though she knew it was only a story, Cammie shivered. Jess's voice sounded really spooky!

"The ghost of the crotchety crab came closer and closer," whispered Jess. "Whe-ere is my missing claw? Whe-ere is my missing claw...?" Everyone leaned forward, straining to hear. Even Cora was listening now, her eyes wide.

"YOU'VE GOT IT!" shouted Jess suddenly, whirling about and grabbing Fizz's tail.

Everyone screeched in surprise, Fizz the loudest of all! When they saw the big grin on Jess's face they started laughing so hard that they made waves in the water...except for Corinetta, who just looked cross at having been taken in.

"That's not really a *proper* ghost story," she sniffed.

"It'll do for us," smiled Miss Swish. "Come on, everyone, time for bed!"

Snuggling up on her seaweed bed later, Cammie thought about everything that had happened. She'd thought she knew so much about camping, but she hadn't really known anything at all! If only she had listened to Miss Swish from the start, she'd have done much better.

I won't make the same mistake when I try for my pearl, she promised herself as she drifted off to sleep. *In the next two weeks, I'm going to find out everything about camping that I can!*

Chapter Six

"My, you've been doing a lot of reading!" exclaimed Miss Sand, the librarian. It was a week later, and Cammie was returning a stack of shell-books to the Rainbow Reef Library.

Cammie nodded. "Do you have anything else about camping?" she asked hopefully as

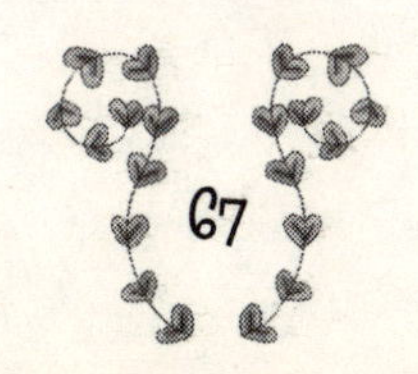

a crab assistant scuttled up. Taking the books, he quickly scurried away again.

Miss Sand thought for a moment. "Yes, but they're for older seahorses. You might find them a bit hard going."

Cammie gulped when Miss Sand showed her the thick titles. They'd take her ages to read! Still, she needed to find out all she could...and those books certainly looked like they had a lot of information.

"I'll take them," decided Cammie. She pulled the books off the shelf. "Oof!" she grunted. They weighed a ton!

"Are you going to be all right with those?" asked Miss Sand.

Cammie nodded, clutching the heavy books with her tail. "Thanks, Miss Sand!" she said, and swam slowly off, wobbling her way through the library doors.

"You're no fun at all any more," complained Tigg. She swam in bored circles around Cammie. "All you ever do now is read."

"Mmm," said Cammie as she turned a page.

Tigg got a naughty gleam in her eye. Swimming closer, she blew bubbles in Cammie's ear.

"Tigg! Leave me alone!" squealed Cammie, slamming her book shut. She wished that she didn't have to share a bedroom with her little sister. She could be such a pest at times!

"Fine," said Tigg. "I'll go and find Stripe. *He's* more fun than you, even if he is a boy!" She sped off with her nose in the air.

Cammie sighed as she opened her book again. Tigg was right; she hadn't been much fun lately. But though she'd been studying so hard, she wasn't sure it was helping. These books used so many big words! They made camping seem very complicated.

I'll just have to try harder, thought Cammie worriedly. *We're trying for our pearl in a few days!* With a tired yawn, she started to read once more. If she could only get her pearl, it would all be worth it.

At last the day arrived. "Is everyone ready?" smiled Miss Swish. Cammie's heart beat hard as she and Jess exchanged a glance. The time to try for their pearls had finally come.

"Good," said Miss Swish. She flicked her pale-green tail. "Come along, then, Dancing Waves – single swim!"

Just as they had before, the seahorses

swam off in a long line. But this time Cammie hardly even noticed the beauty of the Reef. She was too busy trying to remember everything she had read. She frowned nervously as she swam along.

"Don't worry," whispered Jess, swimming close to her. "You'll do fine."

"I hope so," Cammie murmured back. "But Jess...what if I mess everything up again?"

"You won't," said her friend firmly. "I bet you know more about camping than Miss Swish by now!"

Corinetta drew up beside them. "Oh, I can hardly *wait* to get my pearl," she said with a sigh, tossing her golden head. "Some of us are certain to, you know."

"Don't be silly. No one's *certain* to," pointed out Bree, who had overheard. Cammie was surprised to see that the clever seahorse looked worried, too.

"Well, some of us are a lot more certain to than others!" said Corinetta. She smirked at

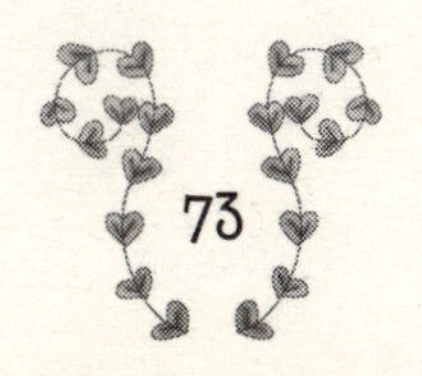

Cammie, and then swam away. Cammie glared after her, her cheeks hot.

"Don't pay any attention," said Jess. "I don't know what she's acting so sandy for – her campsite wasn't that great either!"

Finally Miss Swish stopped. They had reached a large piece of blue coral, peppered with caves. "Here we are," she said. "You each have one hour to prepare your campsite and start your dinner. Ready?"

Everyone nodded. Even Corinetta seemed a bit uneasy now.

"Then GO," called Miss Swish. "And good luck!"

The others swam off quickly. Cammie started to follow...but then she hesitated. What size cave should she choose? The books she had read all said different things. Some thought a small cave was best, and some said a large one was better.

Jess swam back to her. "What's wrong?" she asked, bobbing up and down in the water.

"Nothing," said Cammie. "I'm just trying to decide what size cave I need."

"Well, you'd better do it quickly," urged Jess. "We've only got an hour!" She zoomed off again in a blue-green blur.

Cammie knew that her friend was right, which made her even more nervous than before. She swam from cave to cave, peering into them. What if she chose a small cave, and Miss Swish said a large one would have been better? But if she took a large one, then Miss

Swish might shake her head and say it should have been small.

With alarm, Cammie saw that the others had all chosen their caves. Fizz and Bree were even fishing already!

I'll try to find a medium-sized one, decided Cammie. But by then, all the medium-sized caves had been taken. Cammie turned on her tail, staring fretfully around her. What should she do?

Corinetta swam past, carrying a pile of seaweed. "What's wrong, Cammie?" she asked sweetly. "Having trouble?"

"No," said Cammie quickly. "I'm just – er – thinking, that's all!" She sped away before Corinetta could reply. She was sure that she heard the other seahorse sniggering at her.

Maybe there are more medium-sized caves further along, thought Cammie. She raced to the far end of the coral, sending shoals of silvery fish scattering away in alarm.

Yet none of these caves seemed right, either. Every time Cammie thought she'd found one, a line from one of her books would pop into her head…and then she'd realize that it was too rocky, or too narrow, or too dark.

This is impossible! thought Cammie, swimming from cave to cave. They all had something wrong with them. How had the others managed to find caves so quickly?

In a panic, Cammie swam back to the first cave she'd seen. This one would just have to do. Now, what was next? Sweeping, that was it! Hastily, she began sweeping the sandy floor clean with her tail.

But she had hardly even begun when she heard Miss Swish calling. "Cammie? Cammie! Where are you?"

Chapter Seven

"Here, Miss Swish," replied Cammie, popping her head out of the cave.

The Dancing Waves leader came swimming up. "I didn't expect you to camp so far away!" she exclaimed. "I've been looking all over for you. Have you finished your campsite?"

Cammie's heart thudded. An hour *couldn't*

have passed already...could it? "No, I – I'm just getting started," she admitted. "Have I run out of time?"

"I'm afraid so," said Miss Swish kindly. "The others all finished a while ago, and are cooking their stews."

Cammie swallowed hard, trying to hold back the tears. "You mean...I won't get my pearl?" she whispered.

Miss Swish shook her head. "Not this time, I'm afraid. I'm sorry, Cammie, but Seahorse Stars need to be able to make camp quickly. What took you so long?"

Cammie told her. The Pearlie leader looked surprised. "But Cammie, any of these caves would have been fine! It sounds like you were trying too hard, and got your tail in a twist.

Don't worry, though. You can have another go in a few weeks."

A few weeks? Cammie swallowed hard, trying not to cry. How could she bear it, being the only Dancing Wave without a pearl? She'd feel like such a loser!

"Come on, let's go back to the others," said Miss Swish gently. "You don't want to stay out here on your own. Since your camp isn't finished yet, you can share with one of the other girls tonight."

"Okay," mumbled Cammie.

Miss Swish patted her on the shoulder. "Don't worry, I'm sure you'll get your pearl next time."

Cammie swam along after Miss Swish, feeling very discouraged. She had tried so hard, and it had still been a disaster. It was starting to look as if she and camping were a hopeless combination.

And if she couldn't earn her camping pearl...then she'd never get to be a Seahorse Star after all.

* * *

Cammie tried to put on a cheerful face when they got back to the others, but it wasn't easy. She stared wistfully at the single, gleaming pearl that they all wore on their crowns. The pearl-coloured bead that she wore around her neck seemed very babyish now.

Corinetta tossed her golden head, looking smug. "What did I say?" she demanded. "I knew *I* would get my pearl. Some seahorses were just meant to be Seahorse Stars!"

"She was the last one to finish," whispered Jess in Cammie's ear. "*And* she almost forgot to tidy her bed again. She had to rush in and do it at the last minute, when Miss Swish wasn't looking!"

Cammie knew that Jess was trying to cheer

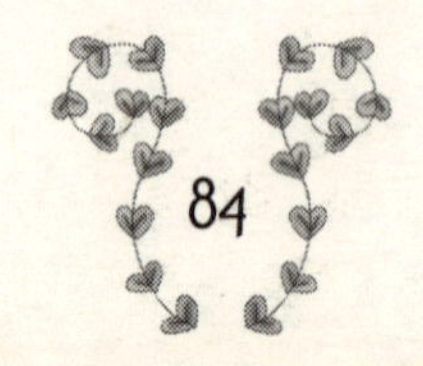

her up, but it didn't help very much. Even if Corinetta hadn't done as well as the others, she had still earned her pearl!

Cammie shared Jess's cave that night. She curled up sadly on the bed of soft seaweed. She had never dreamed that being a Pearlie would be so difficult.

The next morning Cammie saw Miss Swish look worriedly at the sky far above the Reef. It was dark and grey, and the water felt choppy around them.

"Girls, I think we'd better go home now," she said. "I had planned on taking you to see the Crystal Caves today, but that can wait for another time. There's a storm brewing!"

A storm! Hastily, the young seahorses

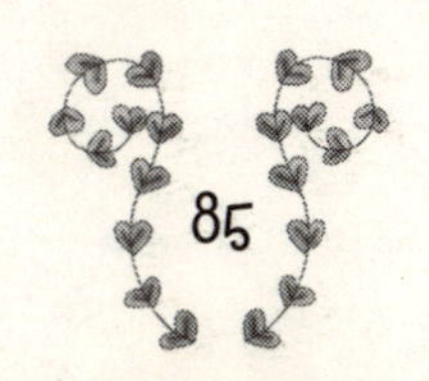

packed their camping gear back into their rucksacks. Cammie glumly fastened hers shut. Soon she'd have to tell her family that she hadn't got her pearl after all. They'd be so disappointed!

"Hurry, girls," urged Miss Swish.

Leaving the coral behind, the seahorses started home again, with Miss Swish in the lead. Suddenly lightning flashed far overhead. Rain lashed down, and the water began churning around them. Cammie held back a shriek as she struggled to swim. The water was tossing them about like grains of sand.

"Anchor down, everybody!" called Miss Swish, shouting to be heard over the storm. "Find a blade of eelgrass and hang on to it – we'll have to wait it out!"

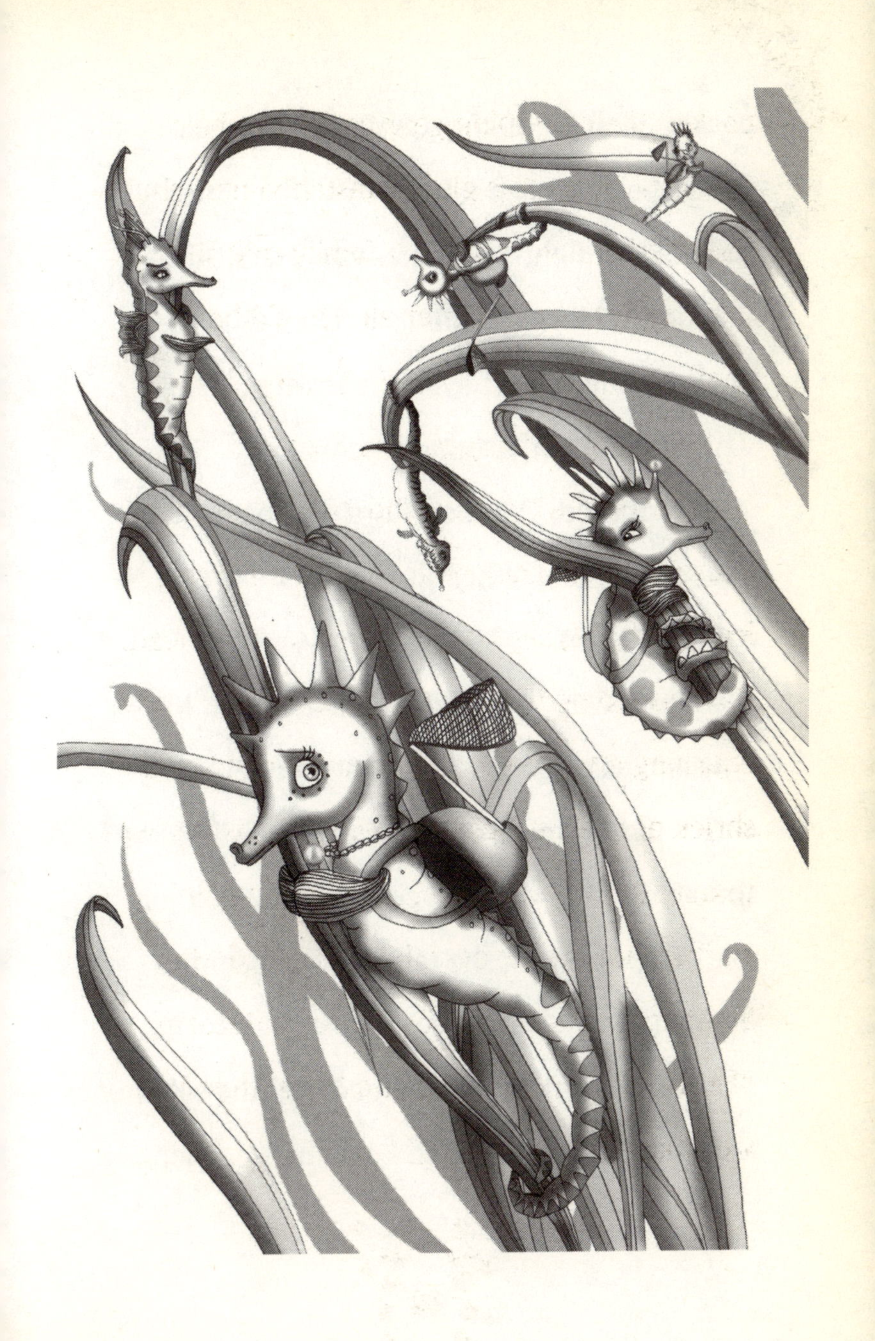

Her heart thudding, Cammie spotted a piece of eelgrass nearby. She grabbed onto it, and held on tightly with her tail. The other girls did the same. Cammie noticed that they all looked a bit pale, even the fearless Fizz. The storm raged around them.

"I'm scared!" sobbed Cora. For once, nobody laughed at her. Everyone else was frightened, too.

"Don't worry, we'll be fine!" shouted Miss Swish. "Just hold on tightly, everyone!"

Soon, Cammie's blade of grass was lashing about so wildly that she could barely hold on to it. To her alarm, she felt her grip begin to weaken.

"Miss Swish!" she screamed, but the storm was so loud now that she knew her teacher couldn't hear her. She gritted her teeth, struggling to hang on. Her tail slipped a bit – and then another bit—

"Agh!" shrieked Cammie as the storm suddenly tore her away from the eelgrass. And then she was swept away, tumbling head over fins through the water!

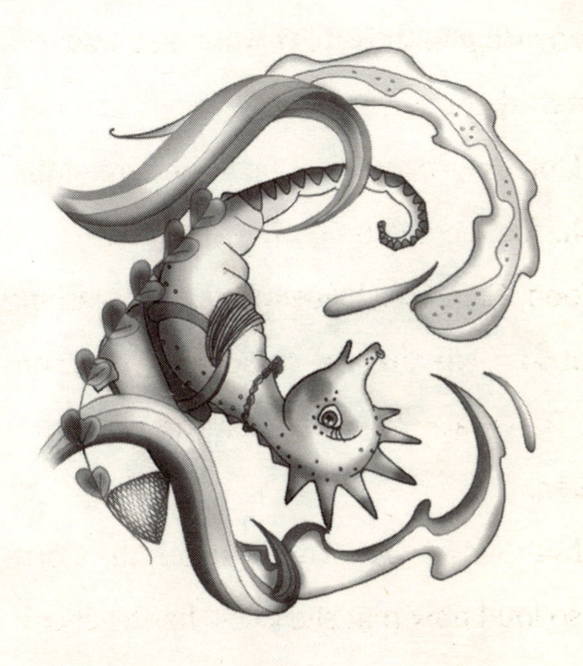

Cammie closed her eyes tightly as she was tossed and turned. The waves roared around her. Finally, just when she thought it would never end, the world grew calm again.

Cautiously, Cammie opened her eyes, and then gasped in dismay. She was in a part of the Reef she'd never seen before…and Miss Swish and the others were nowhere to be seen!

Chapter Eight

Cammie turned on her tail, staring at the strange rocks and corals. What was she going to do? A frightened lump grew in her throat. She wanted her mum and dad!

"Oh, great – it's *you*," said a sulky voice nearby.

Cammie whirled about in the water. There,

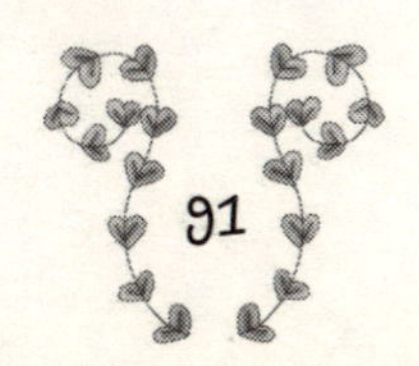

swimming towards her, was a very bedraggled-looking seahorse with a single pearl on her golden crown. It was Corinetta!

Cammie gaped at her. "What are *you* doing here?" she asked.

The other seahorse huffed out an irritated breath. "Same as you, I suppose. The storm carried me away. Ick, it's got me feeling all topsy-turvy! Do you know where we are?"

Cammie shook her head.

Corinetta's sour expression grew even sourer. "Perfect! Me neither." She sniffed. "You know, I *really* think Miss Swish might have thought of this before she took us camping."

"But it wasn't Miss Swish's fault!" exclaimed Cammie. "She didn't cause the storm."

Corinetta pulled a face. "Maybe, but she still should have known it might happen. My mum and dad aren't going to be pleased at all."

Cammie held back a groan. Of all the seahorses in the Dancing Waves, *why* did she have to get stuck with Corinetta? "Well...what are we going to do?" she asked worriedly.

Corinetta looked surprised. "Do? I'm not going to do anything! I'm going to wait here until someone comes and rescues me."

All at once Cammie remembered something that Miss Swish had told them: *If you ever find yourself in a strange place, the first thing you should do is build a campsite!*

But when she said this to Corinetta, the golden seahorse just sneered at her. "A campsite? Oh, and I suppose you want me to do all the work, since *you* don't know how."

"I do not!" cried Cammie, stung. "I just thought—"

"Well, forget it," snapped Corinetta. "*You* make a campsite – if you can! I don't see why

I should bother, when none of this was my fault in the first place." And with that, she plunked herself down onto a seashell and stuck her nose in the air.

Cammie glared at her. Fine! She'd probably get it done faster without Corinetta's help, anyway.

Crossly, she swam over to the nearby coral, where there were some caves. *That one*, she decided, after checking first that there weren't any crab tracks in front of it. Soon she had swept the cave out neatly, and was gathering seaweed for a bed.

Corinetta watched with a superior smirk. "I really don't know why you're bothering," she scoffed. "We can't be *that* lost. Someone will be here any second now."

"I hope so," said Cammie, gathering seaweed in her tail. "But Miss Swish said you should always build a campsite in a strange place, so that's what I'm doing. And if no one *does* come, then at least I'll have a place to sleep tonight!"

Corinetta's smug look wavered for a moment. Then she recovered herself. "Oh, don't be ridiculous!" she said, turning away.

Finishing her bed, Cammie took her fishing net from her rucksack and began to fish for plankton. This time, she remembered to hold the net further away from her. Soon she had a nice, big catch. She smiled triumphantly.

Then she started on her stew, mixing the plankton with bits of tasty seaweed and sea-spices. She even found a bit of wild sea lettuce growing nearby. She carefully stirred it in, remembering that her father had often bragged that this was his secret ingredient.

After a while, Corinetta appeared at the mouth of the cave. She peered inside, looking hungry. "Oh, you've made a stew," she said in a casual voice.

"Would you like some?" asked Cammie.

"Well – I *suppose* I could help you eat it," said Corinetta grandly. "It looks like you've made way too much."

"Thanks," said Cammie, rolling her eyes. Trust Corinetta to make it sound like she was doing her a favour!

Corinetta swam into the cave, swishing her tail. "Not bad," she said as she took a bite. "Of course, it's nothing like *my* stew."

"Isn't it?" said Cammie. She held back a laugh. Corinetta's stew the night before had been so bad that she had eaten most of Cora's instead!

The two girls were halfway through their

meal when Cammie heard a voice calling. "Cammie! Corinetta! Where are you?"

"Miss Swish!" gasped Cammie. She raced to the cave's entrance. "We're here, we're here!" she yelled.

Corinetta looked smug as Miss Swish spotted them and started swimming in their direction. "See, I told you," she boasted. "I knew there was no need to make a campsite."

Before Cammie could reply, Miss Swish came speeding up. "Oh, thank heavens – I've been so worried about you both!" She stopped suddenly, looking about her in surprise. "Why, what a good campsite!" she exclaimed. "Did you do this, Corinetta?"

Cammie's jaw dropped. *Corinetta?*

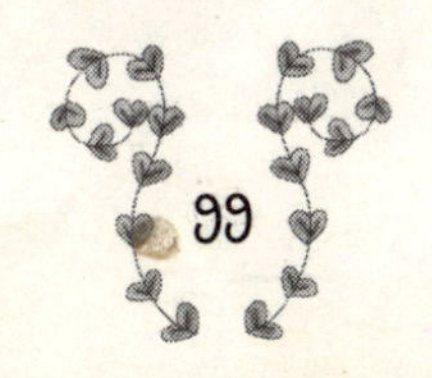

The golden seahorse didn't deny it. She gave a smirk, swishing her tail. "Well..."

"I'm glad to see you made a campsite when you found yourself in a strange place," said Miss Swish approvingly. "This is very nicely done, Corinetta. I like how tidy your bed looks – and your stew smells delicious!"

"But she *didn't* do it!" burst out Cammie. "It was me, not her!" She felt close to tears. How could Corinetta take credit for her campsite? She hadn't even lifted a fin to help!

Corinetta's cheeks turned pink as she scowled at her. "Ha!" she blustered. "As if *you* could make a campsite. Why, you don't even have a camping pearl!"

"Girls, that's enough!" broke in Miss Swish. "Are you *both* saying that you're

the one who made this campsite?"

Cammie nodded vehemently. Corinetta hesitated only a moment before she nodded, too.

Miss Swish looked taken aback. Then her gaze fell on the pot of plankton stew. Swimming over to it, she tried a bite. "Mm, delicious!" she said. "And I think I can taste a rather unusual ingredient in it, too. Corinetta, do you know what it is?"

Corinetta squirmed. "Um...I don't really remember. I – I just threw in all sorts of things."

"It's sea lettuce!" cried Cammie eagerly. "My dad always puts it in *his* stew. He says it's his secret ingredient, so I thought I'd try it, too."

Miss Swish smiled at her. "Well, he's right – it's very tasty!" Her expression turned serious as she looked back at Corinetta. "You didn't make this campsite at all, did you, Corinetta?" she asked.

"No," admitted the golden seahorse

sullenly. "I was only kidding, that's all. It's not my fault Cammie can't take a joke."

"It's hardly a joke to try and take credit for someone else's work," said Miss Swish sternly. "That's not how a good Pearlie behaves, Corinetta!" As Corinetta scowled down at the sand, Miss Swish turned back to Cammie.

"Well done, my dear!" she said. "I'm sorry I didn't realize that the campsite was yours at first. But you see? When you didn't stop and confuse yourself with all those different opinions, you were able to do a first-rate job!"

Cammie realized in surprise that this was true. In fact, she had been so cross with Corinetta that she had hardly stopped to think at all – yet somehow, she'd known exactly what to do!

"You've shown that you can make an excellent campsite, and quickly too," went on Miss Swish. "I think you deserve to earn your camping pearl for this."

"*Really?*" gasped Cammie. She was so excited that she shot up towards the ceiling.

Miss Swish laughed. "Really!"

"But that's not fair—" Corinetta started. Then she saw Miss Swish scowling at her. "I mean – erm – well done, Cammie. Sorry for teasing you." She gave her a sickly-sweet smile.

"Come here, Cammie, and I'll give you your pearl," said Miss Swish.

Hardly able to believe this was happening, Cammie swam forward. With great ceremony, Miss Swish took a gleaming white pearl from

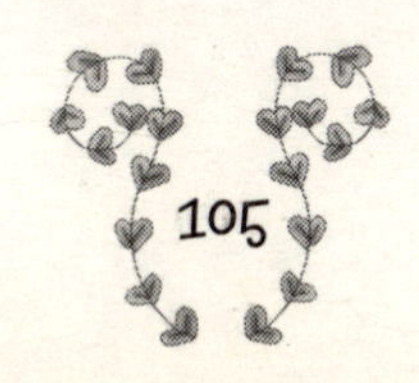

the bag at her hip and placed it on one of the points of Cammie's crown.

"I'm delighted to award you your camping pearl, Cammie," she said warmly. "Congratulations – you're on your way to being a Seahorse Star!"

"Thank you!" cried Cammie. She felt so happy that she thought she might burst.

"And as for *you*, Corinetta..." Miss Swish shook her head. "I want you to think very hard about the Pearlie Rule: to think of others before yourself, and do a good turn every day. I think you might find that you need to work on it!"

"Yes, Miss Swish," mumbled Corinetta.

"Now then, let's go home, girls," said Miss Swish. "And Cammie – congratulations again!

You've worked hard, and you deserve your pearl."

"Thank you," said Cammie shyly. She looked around the tidy cave with pride. How good to know that she could make her own campsite whenever she needed to now, just like a real Seahorse Star!

Soon they were heading for home, with Miss Swish in the lead. Corinetta lagged sulkily behind.

Cammie felt fizzy with excitement at the thought of showing Jess her pearl. Her best friend would be thrilled! Not to mention how pleased her parents would be.

I'm the luckiest seahorse in the world, thought Cammie happily. Not only did she live in a beautiful place like Rainbow Reef, but she was also a Pearlie...and she had a glistening white pearl on her crown. She could hardly wait to try for her next one!

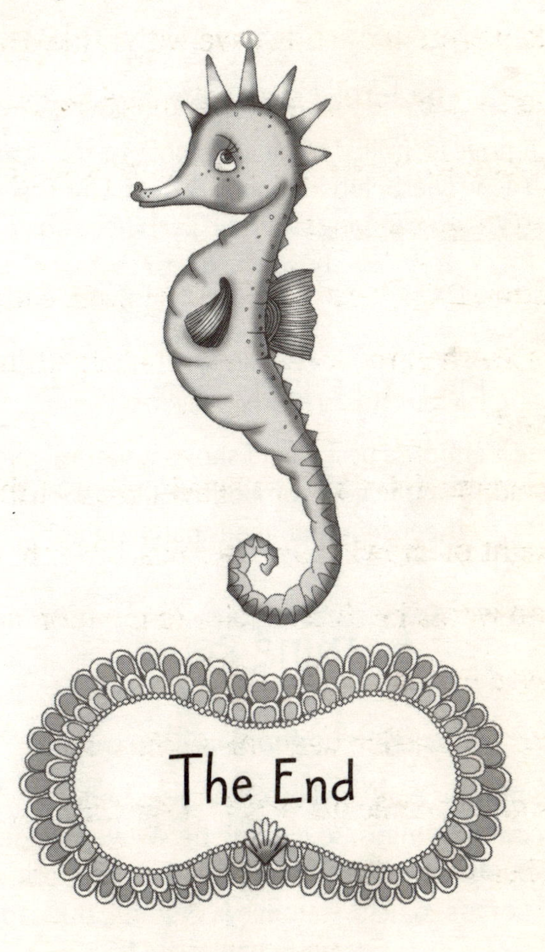

Dive in with Cammie and her friends and collect every splash-tastic tale in

Seahorse Stars!

The First Pearl

ISBN 9781409520245

Cammie is thrilled to be a member of the Pearlies – the waviest club in Rainbow Reef. Her first task is to go camping. Will she keep her cool, or is she in too deep?

First-Aid Friends

ISBN 9781409520252

When Cammie's best friend shows a natural talent for first-aid, Cammie gets competitive...and soon it's their friendship that needs patching up!

Coming soon...

The Lost Lagoon

ISBN 9781409520269

Cammie is confused by compasses and lost when it comes to maps, so earning her Wave Wandering Pearl is proving tricky. When stuck-up Corinetta offers to help, Cammie is grateful. But can Corinetta be trusted?

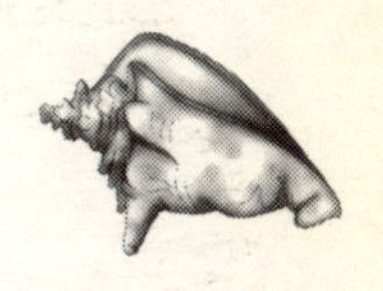

Danger in the Deep

ISBN 9781409520276

Cammie loves studying for her Sea Safety pearl and learning about the dangers of the Deep. So when her little sister disappears, it's up to Cammie to rescue her...

Dancing Waves

ISBN 9781409520306

All the seahorses must work together if they are to earn their Tidal Team pearl...and they've chosen Cammie as their team leader. Can she stop them squabbling and help them come out on top?

The Rainbow Queen

ISBN 9781409520313

To get her last Proficiency Pearl, Cammie must do a good deed in Rainbow Reef...and then she will be a Seahorse Star! But when Cammie begins her task, she realizes the Reef is in danger, and she must ask the Queen for help.

For more wonderfully wavy reads
check out
www.fiction.usborne.com